DISCARDED BY THE
BLANCHESTER PUBLIC LIBRARY

RIDING TO SCHOOL ON MY LITTLE YELLOW SCHOOL BUS

Retold by NICHOLAS IAN

Illustrated by DIEGO FUNCK

Music Produced by ERIK KOSKINEN and RECORDED AT REAL PHONIC STUDIOS

CANTATA LEARNING

WWW.CANTATALEARNING.COM

Blanchester Public Library
110 North Broadway
Blanchester OH 45107
(937) 783-3585

CANTATA LEARNING

Published by Cantata Learning
1710 Roe Crest Drive
North Mankato, MN 56003
www.cantatalearning.com

Copyright © 2017 Cantata Learning

All rights reserved. No part of this publication may be reproduced
in any form without written permission from the publisher.

A note to educators and librarians from the publisher: Cantata Learning has provided the following data to assist in book processing and suggested use of Cantata Learning product.

Publisher's Cataloging-in-Publication Data
Prepared by Librarian Consultant: Ann-Marie Begnaud
Library of Congress Control Number: 2015958190
    Riding to School on My Little Yellow School Bus
    Series: Tangled Tunes : On the Move
    Retold by Nicholas Ian
    Illustrated by Diego Funck
    Summary: How do kids travel from place to place? Do they take a bus, fly in a plane, or ride a horse? Full-color illustrations make this children's song come alive.
    ISBN: 978-1-63290-592-5 (library binding/CD)
    ISBN: 978-1-63290-643-4 (paperback/CD)
Suggested Dewey and Subject Headings:
    Dewey: E 388
    LCSH Subject Headings: Colors – Juvenile literature. | Transportation – Juvenile literature. | Colors – Songs and music – Texts. | Transportation – Songs and music – Texts. | Colors – Juvenile sound recordings. | Transportation – Juvenile sound recordings.
    Sears Subject Headings: Transportation. | Color. | School songbooks. | Children's songs. | Folk music.
    BISAC Subject Headings: JUVENILE NONFICTION / Transportation / General. | JUVENILE NONFICTION / Music / Songbooks. | JUVENILE NONFICTION / Concepts / Colors.

Book design and art direction, Tim Palin Creative
Editorial direction, Flat Sole Studio
Music direction, Elizabeth Draper
Music produced by Erik Koskinen and recorded at Real Phonic Studios

Printed in the United States of America in North Mankato, Minnesota.
072016   0335CGF16

ACCESS THE MUSIC!
SCAN CODE WITH MOBILE APP
CANTATALEARNING.COM

We use many types of **transportation** to get from place to place. We ride a bus to school and pedal a bike to a friend's house. People fly in airplanes to visit family and ride trains to work.

To see how the kids in this song get around, turn the page and sing along!

Let's ride to school!

Riding to school on my little yellow school bus.
Riding to school on my little yellow school bus.
Riding to school on my little yellow school bus,
won't you come along with me?

Riding to the store in my little blue car.
Riding to the store in my little blue car.
Riding to the store in my little blue car,
won't you come along with me?

Get ready to ride your bicycle!

Riding down the path on my little orange bicycle.
Riding down the path on my little orange bicycle.
Riding down the path on my little orange bicycle, won't you come along with me?

Let's ride a horse!

Riding up and down on my little brown horse.
Riding up and down on my little brown horse.
Riding up and down on my little brown horse,
won't you come along with me?

Jump onto the boat!

Riding through the waves on my little white boat.
Riding through the waves on my little white boat.
Riding through the waves on my little white boat, won't you come along with me?

Toot! Toot!

Let's ride in a train!

Riding on the tracks on my little black train.
Riding on the tracks on my little black train.
Riding on the tracks on my little black train, won't you come along with me?

What else can we use to get around?
How about an airplane?

Riding through the air in my little purple airplane.
Riding through the air in my little purple airplane.
Riding through the air in my little purple airplane, won't you come along with me?

Let's take a skateboard ride!

Riding to the park on my little green skateboard.
Riding to the park on my little green skateboard.
Riding to the park on my little green skateboard, won't you come along with me?

Riding all around with you is so much fun!

SONG LYRICS
Riding to School on My Little Yellow School Bus

Let's ride to school!

Riding to school on my little yellow school bus.
Riding to school on my little yellow school bus.
Riding to school on my little yellow school bus,
won't you come along with me?

Hop into the car!

Riding to the store in my little blue car.
Riding to the store in my little blue car.
Riding to the store in my little blue car,
won't you come along with me?

Get ready to ride your bicycle!

Riding down the path on my little orange bicycle.
Riding down the path on my little orange bicycle.
Riding down the path on my little orange bicycle,
won't you come along with me?

Let's ride a horse!

Riding up and down on my little brown horse.
Riding up and down on my little brown horse.
Riding up and down on my little brown horse,
won't you come along with me?

Jump onto the boat!

Riding through the waves on my little white boat.
Riding through the waves on my little white boat.
Riding through the waves on my little white boat,
won't you come along with me?

Toot! Toot!
Let's ride in a train!

Riding on the tracks on my little black train.
Riding on the tracks on my little black train.
Riding on the tracks on my little black train,
won't you come along with me?

What else can we use to get around?
How about an airplane?

Riding through the air in my little purple airplane.
Riding through the air in my little purple airplane.
Riding through the air in my little purple airplane,
won't you come along with me?

Let's take a skateboard ride!

Riding to the park on my little green skateboard.
Riding to the park on my little green skateboard.
Riding to the park on my little green skateboard,
won't you come along with me?

Riding all around with you is so much fun!

Riding to School on My Little Yellow School Bus

Americana
Erik Koskinen

Verse 2
Hop into the car!

Riding to the store in my little blue car.
Riding to the store in my little blue car.
Riding to the store in my little blue car,
won't you come along with me?

Verse 3
Get ready to ride your bicycle!

Riding down the path on my little orange bicycle.
Riding down the path on my little orange bicycle.
Riding down the path on my little orange bicycle,
won't you come along with me?

Verse 4
Let's ride a horse!

Riding up and down on my little brown horse.
Riding up and down on my little brown horse.
Riding up and down on my little brown horse,
won't you come along with me?

Verse 5
Jump onto the boat!

Riding through the waves on my little white boat.
Riding through the waves on my little white boat.
Riding through the waves on my little white boat,
won't you come along with me?

Verse 6
Toot! Toot!
Let's ride in a train!

Riding on the tracks on my little black train.
Riding on the tracks on my little black train.
Riding on the tracks on my little black train,
won't you come along with me?

Verse 7
What else can we use to get around?
How about an airplane?

Riding through the air in my little purple airplane.
Riding through the air in my little purple airplane.
Riding through the air in my little purple airplane,
won't you come along with me?

Verse 8
Let's take a skateboard ride!

Riding to the park on my little green skateboard.
Riding to the park on my little green skateboard.
Riding to the park on my little green skateboard,
won't you come along with me?

Riding all around with you is so much fun!

GLOSSARY

transportation—a way to get around

GUIDED READING ACTIVITIES

1. How do you get to school every day? Draw a picture of yourself on your way to school.

2. How many different ways do people travel in this song? Are there other ways to travel you can think of that weren't in the song?

3. Have you ever been on an airplane or on a boat? What is your favorite way to travel and why?

TO LEARN MORE

Anderson, Steven. *Wheels on the Bus*. Minneapolis: Cantata Learning, 2016.

Lassieur, Allison. *Buses in Action*. North Mankato, MN: Capstone Press, 2012.

Lyons, Shelly. *Transportation in My Neighborhood*. North Mankato, MN: Capstone Press, 2013.

Tourville, Amanda Doering. *Transportation in the City*. Mankato, MN: Capstone Press, 2011.